McWhinney's Jaunt

McWhinney's Jaunt

by *ROBERT LAWSON*

ILLUSTRATIONS BY THE AUTHOR

Little, Brown and Company · Boston · Toronto

FIRST PAPERBACK EDITION

The Library of Congress has cataloged this work as follows:
PZ7
.L4384
Mac   Lawson, Robert, 1892–1957.
                  McWhinney's jaunt. Illus. by the author. [1st ed.]
             Boston, Little, Brown, 1951.
                  76 p.   illus.   22 cm.

             I. Title.
             PZ7.L4384Mac   51-6023 ‡
             Library of Congress   [5]

                              BP

                                /

             *Published simultaneously in Canada
          by Little, Brown & Company (Canada) Limited*

             Printed in the United States of America

To that dear friend
of my youth
BARON KARL FRIEDRICH HIERONYMUS
VON MÜNCHHAUSEN

McWhinney's Jaunt

Mr. Purslane was sitting in his garden resting. He wasn't resting from anything special — just resting.

Suddenly Mr. Purslane was surprised to see a man on a bicycle come riding up the driveway. He was a rather odd-looking man and it was an odd-looking bicycle.

But the strangest thing of all was that most of the time the man was riding through the air, just about a foot or six inches above the surface of the drive.

Each time the tires struck a bump in the driveway the bicycle would bounce up and float along smoothly for fifty feet or so before returning to the gravel.

It seemed most unusual.

Beside the Purslane drive there is an old-fashioned iron hitching post. The stranger rode up to it, snapped one end of a light chain to the ring and dismounted.

As soon as he did so the bicycle rose in the air as far as the chain allowed and hung there, swaying slightly, like a tethered balloon.

The man removed the bicycle clips from his trousers and hung them on the handle bars. He adjusted his old-style round cuffs and walked over to where Mr. Purslane was sitting.

He was not exactly the type of person that one sees every day.

"Good afternoon," he said. "May I introduce myself? The name is McWhinney, Professor Ambrose Augustus McWhinney. Perhaps you have heard of me?"

"No," Mr. Purslane answered, "I don't think I have."

"Don't apologize," the other said. "Few people ever have. Have you ever heard of Z-Gas?"

"No," answered Mr. Purslane, "I never have."

"No need to apologize," said the stranger. "*No* one ever has."

He sat down, removed his hat and polished his forehead with a Persian silk handkerchief. The hat was quite fascinating. It was an ancient, tall, stovepipe model and the band was evidently used for holding useful things.

Stuck in it were: three fishhooks and half a dozen matches, a can opener, a bottle opener, some toothpicks and a New York, New Haven and Hartford timetable. Also an extra pair of spectacles, three pipe cleaners, several calling cards, an eagle feather, a nail file, a rolled-up violin string, needles and thread, a packet of zinnia seeds and the minute hand of a grandfather's clock.

"It just goes to show," the Professor said, "what laziness can do."

*　　　*　　　*

Now I have always been very fond of bicycling (the Professor began), but I disliked pumping up my own tires — just sheer laziness. I decided that it would be far easier to inflate them by means of a pressure tank equipped with a suitable tube.

So in my laboratory I put a great many chemicals together in a heavy steel tank. I will not bother to tell you what they were — you wouldn't understand anyway.

The mixture of these ingredients was supposed to generate a pressure in the tank and, like all my experiments, this one worked perfectly. The gauge on the tank soon indicated an excellent pressure.

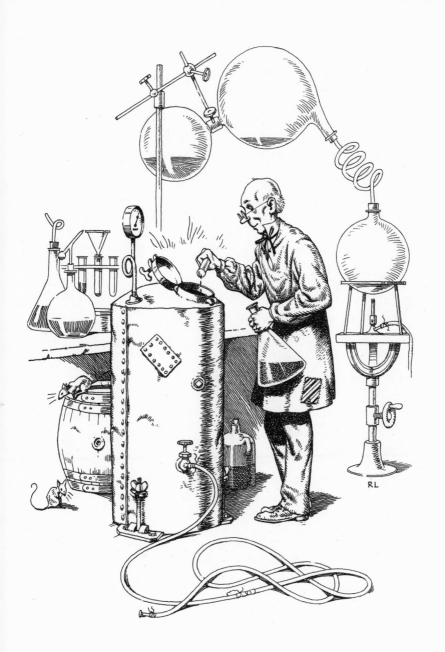

However, when I inflated the tires of my bicycle (they were a new pair and had never been pumped up before), a remarkable thing occurred. The moment that they were filled the bicycle began to rise straight up in the air, despite all my efforts to hold it down.

Luckily there was a light but strong piece of chain nearby and I was able to fasten one end of this to the bicycle and tie the other end to a stout tree.

It was our dog's chain and since he was still attached to it there was a certain amount of confusion.

I at once deduced that the mixture I had made in the tank had not only caused a pressure, but had produced a hitherto unknown gas, having tremendous lifting power.

Of course it was a most important discovery, but as I had already forgotten several of the ingredients it did not greatly advance the cause of Science.

I named it Z-Gas, after the last letter of the alphabet.

I now decided to try riding the bicycle and with some effort managed to pull it down and mount. I found that the weight of my body almost exactly counterbalanced the buoyancy of the tires.

Riding down the driveway of our home was a delightful experience, for every slight bump in the surface would send me into the air and I could glide along for incredible distances before returning to the ground.

It was exactly the same sensation that one often encounters in dreams.

Experimenting further, I discovered that by merely leaning far back in the saddle and pedaling briskly I could rise to almost any height I chose, "gliding through the air," as the song has it, "with the greatest of ease." To descend I simply leaned forward on the handle bars and guided myself back to earth.

I practiced all afternoon with much satisfaction and by evening was able to ride on the earth or through the air with equal facility.

Since it was vacation time at my university and since Mrs. McWhinney, having taken up needlepoint, had become a great bore, I decided that I would benefit by a trip somewhere else. This new discovery seemed to promise a pleasant mode of locomotion. The only impediment was a lack of money, a condition not infrequent in our household.

Recollecting that there was a Carnival in town, I filled a small tank with Z-Gas and placed it in a wheelbarrow. It was necessary to weight it down with several heavy stones.

The Carnival man who operated the balloon concession was greatly interested when I demonstrated the tremendous lifting power of Z-Gas. "That's hot stuff," he exclaimed. "Why, two or three balloons will lift a kid right offen his feet. They'll go for it."

After some chaffering he agreed to pay fifty dollars for a season's supply.

As the gates were then opening, he hastily began to fill a great number of balloons. Suddenly, to his surprise, he started to rise slowly in the air. I shouted to him to release the balloons, but he foolishly held on until it was too late to let go.

When I last saw him he had just cleared the roof of the A & P building and was drifting slowly in a southeasterly direction.

Fortunately he had already paid me.

That evening I packed a few necessities such as underwear, pajamas, toothbrush, pickled peaches, an almanac, an alarm clock and some salted peanuts in the handle-bar baskets, oiled my trusty bicycle and informed Mrs. McWhinney that I was leaving for Hollywood in the morning.

She had run out of magenta thread and was wondering whether green would do just as well, so she paid very little attention.

I had two reasons for choosing Hollywood as my destination. First, I felt that this remarkable bicycle might secure me an engagement in the motion pictures more remunerative than my professorship. Secondly, and this was purely personal, I had hopes of meeting face to face that lovely star Gloria Glamora, who has always typified all my ideals of feminine charm and beauty.

Shortly after sunup I made an early start and was soon skimming down the Murphy Parkway. Of course, as on most parkways, bicycling was strictly forbidden, but whenever I saw a Police car I merely leaned back and soared over it, much to the surprise of the officers.

I avoided all toll booths in the same manner, which, perhaps, was not strictly honest, but with only fifty dollars on which to cross the continent it was necessary to conserve every dime.

I soon reached New York City and was faced by the barrier of the mighty Hudson, but crossing this proved no great difficulty.

Mounting one of the great supporting cables of the George Washington Bridge I pedaled up it to the top of the first tower. It was a rather stiff climb, but once there the view was magnificent.

The coast down the gracefully curving cable was a thrilling experience and the momentum carried me halfway up the farther slope.

Coasting down from the second tower I became aware of several Police cars and a great deal of activity around the toll booth on the New Jersey shore. So I took off part way down the incline and soared well above the booth and almost across the Jersey Meadows before returning to terra firma.

Before long I discovered that heat greatly increased the lifting power of the Z-Gas in my tires. I had already noted that during the warmth of the day it was much easier to ride through the air than in the cool of the morning or evening.

However, in crossing Pennsylvania I had a dramatic demonstration of this which might easily have proved fatal. It was in a district of steel mills, mostly located in ravines and gulleys. To avoid this ugliness I was flying above them when I chanced to pass directly above what appeared to be an idle blast furnace.

Barely had I passed over it when it suddenly erupted a veritable volcano of flame, smoke and soot. I tremble to think of the results had it occurred a second earlier.

As it was I was only slightly singed, but the effect on my tires was alarming. Both of them swelled to the danger point and I rose to a tremendous height. It took an hour or more of violent pedaling to get down to earth again.

It was a terrifying experience and one which I took pains not to repeat.

With such a small amount of capital at my disposal it was necessary to spend my nights in the cheapest lodgings obtainable, usually roadside cabins.

It was my invariable custom to take my bicycle to my room with me. There I would allow it to rise to the ceiling where it remained safely all night, completely out of the way. In a more pretentious hostelry this might have caused some comment, but in the sort of places I was obliged to patronize it passed unnoticed.

One evening, however, the cabin to which I was assigned was so flimsily constructed that when my bicycle pressed against the ceiling the entire roof began to rise up and disintegrate.

Fortunately I managed to catch the mooring chain and attach it to the foot of my bed. Then, with the aid of a sheet, I was able to tie the rear wheel to the head of the bed. But the weight of the bed was not enough to hold down the bicycle without my own weight added, so I dared not remove myself from it the entire night. I was forced to undress sitting up in bed and to retire without brushing my teeth, a thing which always causes me to sleep badly.

All told, it was a most uncomfortable stay.

So far the weather had proved ideal, but as I approached the Middle West the sun became intensely hot and there were occasional showers. I greatly felt the need of some protection from the elements and this was afforded me in an almost providential manner.

An extremely violent rain squall overtook me as I passed through a wealthy suburb of Dayton, Ohio, I believe it was. The wind was terrific and the air was filled with flying objects of various sorts.

Among these I spied exactly what I needed, a handsome lawn umbrella, decorated with orange mermaids. The mermaids were not necessary, but the umbrella was. With great exertions I managed to capture this, close it and fasten it to my bicycle.

I should, perhaps, have turned it in at the Lost and Found Bureau, if there was one, but by the time the storm had abated I had been blown many miles beyond the town. So I felt no qualms of conscience about retaining this most useful piece of equipment.

Moreover, I felt that people should take better care of their property and not allow it to be blown about the streets, gravely endangering the safety of innocent passers-by.

The umbrella proved to be of great value, not only because of its shelter from the weather, but also as an assistance in locomotion.

For the top was adjustable, so when there was a favoring wind I had merely to adjust it to the correct angle and the breeze propelled me at a splendid rate, with no effort at all on my part.

The only difficulty lay in the fact that when set at certain angles the umbrella cut off my view of approaching objects and I had several narrow escapes from serious accidents. I soon remedied this, however, by cutting a small window which I covered with cellophane.

I also attached to the edge of the umbrella a lightweight canvas curtain which, of course, was looped up during the day, but at night could be lowered to the ground, forming a neat circular tent that sheltered my bicycle, myself and my belongings.

Later, in the Great Open Spaces of the Far West, I found this most useful.

I found Ohio, Indiana and Illinois rather tiresome, being mostly corn. However, the roads were flat and straight and the wind, though hot, blew strongly from the east. With the aid of my umbrella I passed through them quite quickly, skimming over all cars which impeded my progress and only touching the earth every few miles.

I crossed the Mississippi, known as the Father of Waters, at St. Louis, riding over the upper girders of the famed Municipal Bridge. This was during the evening rush hour and the sight of me and my bicycle crossing in this unconventional manner seemed to cause some little confusion in the motor traffic. Several Police cars blew their sirens at me, but as they also were caught in the jam they were helpless to follow.

I found Missouri as tiresome as Ohio, Indiana and Illinois, being also mostly corn.

By now my finances were depleted almost to the vanishing point. While considering what could be done to better my condition I chanced upon a County Fair being held in some Missouri hamlet, the name of which I have forgotten.

I was about to pass it by when my eye was caught by a large banner announcing a Grand Championship Bicycle Race, for a purse of $500.

Entering the grounds I discovered that the race was about to start and that the entry fee was two dollars. It was a grave decision which confronted me, for at the moment my entire fortune consisted of $2.17, but without hesitation I stepped up, paid my fee and was entered for the race.

Most of the contestants seemed to be professional riders and eyed me and my bicycle with ill-concealed contempt.

I hastily detached the umbrella and the two baskets which contained my belongings and placed them in the care of a kindly bystander. Since the other riders all wore very scanty costumes I also doffed my hat and removed my outer garments, entrusting them to the same person.

Then I strode determinedly up to the starting line.

Not being accustomed to professional racing I got off to a rather poor start. Each of the other contestants had a handler who held the bicycle while he mounted and at the sound of the gun gave him a great push.

Of course I was not so equipped and by the time I had mounted and gotten started all the others were well down the track, bunched in a tight group.

I pedaled briskly and thanks to the Z-Gas in my tires, which enabled me to skim along so lightly, soon overhauled the pack.

However, it now appeared that they had entered into a dastardly conspiracy, for every time I attempted to pass, they grouped themselves closely directly in front of me, completely blocking my progress. At the same time they turned around, jeering and making insulting remarks.

Angered by such bad sportsmanship I thereupon dropped back a short distance, pedaled hard, leaned back in the saddle, pulled up on the handle bars and skimmed swiftly over their heads, landing well down the track ahead of them. I could now really make speed and soon caught up to the pack again and repeated the performance.

The race was one mile, or four times around the track, and in that distance I managed to lap the field (as the expression has it) twice, and to cross the finish line several hundred feet ahead of the nearest contender.

Such a feat had never before been witnessed and of course the ovation was tremendous. The other contestants, their managers and handlers all protested loudly, but the Judges decided that, although my style of riding was perhaps slightly unorthodox, there was no rule actually forbidding it. I was, therefore, awarded a blue ribbon and, far more important to me, the prize of $500 cash.

I pinned the ribbon to my umbrella and reattached that and the baskets to my bicycle. I also donned my clothing, carefully pinning the money in my vest pocket.

Having rewarded the kindly bystander with a handsome box of cigars which the Mayor had enthusiastically pressed on me, I remounted and amid the plaudits of the throng rode out of the Fairgrounds and resumed my journey.

Now that my financial situation was improved I looked forward to spending my nights in the best hotels, but unfortunately there weren't any. I had now reached the Great Open Spaces, where hotels of any sort were few and far between, and those that there were, were usually crowded to capacity. In one case this exposed me to a most humiliating experience.

In some small Oklahoma oil town, the hotel being filled, I had pitched my tent in a small park opposite the courthouse. In the morning I was awakened by a great deal of jostling and loud talk outside my tent.

Emerging to learn the cause of this I discovered that some enterprising citizen had hung up a sign which read: "See the HOMO SAPIENS — 10¢ a look."

He had arranged several soapboxes so that his ignorant victims could step up and peer down through the window of the umbrella, thus viewing the interior of my tent and my sleeping form. He had apparently been doing a thriving business.

What puzzled me was why none of these dupes protested at being so outrageously fleeced, but they all seemed perfectly well satisfied, indeed many appeared highly amused.

I was glad to leave Oklahoma behind, for not only was the humor of its inhabitants of a low caliber, but it proved to be a very oily state. The roads were always slippery with oil, and riding through the air was a matter of constantly dodging oil derricks.

Moreover new wells, or "gushers," were continually spouting, sending down showers of mud, water and black oil. I was indeed grateful for the protection afforded by my umbrella, but the orange mermaids became sadly spotted and took on the unpleasant appearance of a bad case of smallpox.

Now I was in the heart of the Great West, so famed in song and story. The sweeping plains of Texas, New Mexico and Arizona, the deserts and the dramatic canyons, while doubtless attractive to cattle and Gila Monsters, would have proved a great trial to the ordinary bicyclist.

But the intense heat of the sun lent such buoyancy to my tires that I was enabled to rise to considerable heights, and, with the aid of my umbrella-sail, to travel incredible distances in a day.

Having provided myself with an ample supply of canned goods I usually camped out at night and those nights in the open are among my most treasured memories.

The air was cool and crisp, the stars brilliant. Here one could really relax, safe from all intrusion save an occasional mountain lion or rattlesnake, attracted by the cozy warmth of my tent. Lulled by the sleepy lowing of the cattle and the howl of the distant coyote, I slept as never before.

It also saved considerable expense.

The rest of the journey across these plains and deserts was fairly uneventful, except for one rather startling experience.

It occurred over a most wild and arid stretch of desert. The terrific heat had raised me to a great height and I was floating along easily, not paying much attention to anything. I idly noted some odd-looking steel erections which looked strangely out of place in this desolate waste. One, especially, had the appearance of a shiny metal factory chimney.

Just as I was approaching there was a tremendous explosion and with a terrific roar this huge affair took off and rose swiftly into the upper air, leaving a trail of smoke, flame and vapor.

Luckily I was sufficiently alert to swerve sharply and avoid its course, otherwise I might have sustained serious injury.

It later occurred to me that I must have been over the Government's rocket proving ground at White Sands, New Mexico, a spot which I would strongly advise other travelers to avoid.

I was now approaching that most stupendous of all scenic wonders, the Grand Canyon of the Colorado. Although I had often read of it, no amount of reading or any number of pictures could really prepare one for its breath-taking beauty.

The hotel at which I stopped, located close to the edge of the chasm, was a magnificent affair and extremely expensive. Most of the guests were too.

While my finances were still in excellent shape I did wish to have an ample supply of money on arriving in Hollywood. I therefore engaged in conversation with several of the wealthy gentlemen guests and after a time rather casually led up to the boast that I could ride my bicycle across the Canyon on a kite string.

Of course this was met with a great deal of scoffing and many heavy witticisms. However, as they were all bored, there being nothing to do except look at the scenery, the prospect of any sort of sporting event appealed to them greatly. Within a few moments they had collected a purse of $1000, this to be my reward should I succeed.

I set twelve noon of the following day as the hour for the attempt, since I wanted my tires to have their maximum buoyancy. The Canyon looked awfully deep.

The next morning I managed to procure a couple of miles of light string such as children use in flying kites. Getting it across to the other side of the Canyon presented a problem, but one of the guests who had his private aeroplane kindly flew me across. On the far rim I drove a stout stake, tied the string to it and then we flew back, paying out the string as we came. Here I drove another stake, pulled the string as taut as possible and made it fast.

By now many of the lady guests, convinced that my coming attempt was sheer suicide, protested to the Manager of the hotel, demanding that he stop it. He, however, merely shrugged and said that "the guest is always right." He also added that since I had paid my bill in advance he had nothing to worry about.

They thereupon telephoned to the Sheriff who lived some ninety miles away. He promised to come as quickly as possible, but feared he could not make it before one o'clock.

Everything being prepared I went to my room where I shaved, sent a picture post card to Mrs. McWhinney, oiled my bicycle thoroughly and then took a short nap.

When I emerged and mounted my bicycle promptly at noon the excitement and arguments among the assembled crowd were intense, but my calm, confident air seemed to quiet them somewhat.

All the waiters, bellboys, kitchen help and chambermaids from the hotel were there, as well as the guests, so there was quite a throng. Through this a straight path had been cleared to the edge of the Canyon.

Fearing that the Sheriff might arrive at any moment and spoil everything, I wasted no time but pedaled briskly toward the brink, being careful to ride exactly on the string.

As I neared that awesome gulf many of the ladies screamed and not a few fainted, but all broke into cries of wonder as, without faltering, I continued to ride smoothly out into the air, apparently on the flimsy kite string.

My only difficulty was in staying near enough to the string to make it appear that I was riding on it. For it was swayed by a slight breeze and at times was ten or twenty feet to one side or the other of my tires. However the string was so light that no eye could follow it for more than a few hundred feet and the illusion apparently was perfect.

Reaching the far side, I turned around and came back in the same manner, receiving a tremendous ovation on my return.

I was overwhelmed with attentions, the very ladies who had attempted to prevent my exhibition now hailing me as a superman. Everyone wished to examine my bicycle, but could discover nothing unusual about it. Naturally, I made no mention of the Z-Gas.

In the midst of the excitement the Sheriff arrived, but as I had obviously committed no offense he had no duty to perform. He was most pleasant about it all and was invited to a gala luncheon, provided by the management.

At this luncheon I was formally presented with the $1000 purse and was, of course, called on for a speech. I gave a short talk on "The Effect of Nuclear Fission on the Propagation of the Delphinium," a subject about which I knew nothing and my audience still less.

The Manager attempted to persuade me to remain for the rest of the season and repeat my feat daily. He made most flattering offers of free accommodation and a handsome salary, but my mind being set on Hollywood and higher things, I refused firmly.

Bidding farewell to him, the Sheriff, the generous sportsmen who had provided the purse and, of course, the ladies, I remounted my bicycle and continued on my way.

A few days later found me coasting down a long slope into Hollywood, the fabulous goal of so many hopeful young hearts, the El Dorado of many a fortune seeker, the Mecca of art and beauty. It looked very much like Newark, N.J., only sprawlier.

I secured quarters in a magnificent hostelry abounding in patios, pools, palms, lovebirds, fountains, tropical fish and tourists. The rates were fantastic, but I was well supplied with money and felt it wise to present a certain appearance of affluence.

I had feared that perhaps such an elegant inn might look askance at my parking my bicycle on the ceiling, but the bellboy who showed me to my quarters seemed completely disinterested. "You see everything here," he shrugged. "The last guy was a stilt-walker and always come in through the window, the one before that had a trained hyena."

My quarters were indeed luxurious. In addition to everything else there was a private balcony, which afforded a splendid view of the hotel's swimming pool and the parking lot back of the Super Market.

Reminded that for the past three days I had been traversing hot and dusty deserts I donned my bathing suit, which I had thoughtfully brought along, and enjoyed a most relaxing dip.

To meet a motion picture executive was, of course, my first problem. In my case, unlike the experiences of so many hopefuls, it proved quite simple.

An old colleague of mine, a former Professor of Physics at Harvard, now had an excellent position as an electrician with one of the larger companies. He was well acquainted with Arturo McPhysh, the famous Director, being a member of the same chess club. He gladly arranged an appointment for me with Mr. McPhysh.

Observing that my dress was somewhat somber compared to the colorful garb of the motion picture colony, I added a few Hollywood touches to my costume — a checked sport jacket, a gaily colored scarf and, of course, sunglasses.

Thus spruced up I mounted my bicycle and proceeded to the offices of Superart Masterpieces Inc. to keep my appointment with Mr. McPhysh.

My appointment was for 10:15 A.M. and I was not kept waiting unduly long, Mr. McPhysh emerging from his office promptly at 5:30 P.M.

He led me to one of the outdoor stages and asked that I perform. The stage was being prepared for a historical drama and was mostly occupied by a mammoth reproduction of the Roman Colosseum or the walls of Jericho, I could not quite tell which.

I rode about, skimming lightly over tables, sawhorses, piles of lumber and other things which encumbered the stage, executed a few graceful figures in the air and returned.

"Is that all?" the Director asked, lighting a cigar.

Somewhat nettled I pedaled hard, leaned far back and soared to the top of the great scenic construction. I rode along the crenelated walls, zoomed down through a huge arch, lighted on top of an enormous plaster elephant, rode a telephone wire to the office building and back, and came down with a flourish.

"There's nothing there we couldn't do with mirrors and a couple of wires," Mr. McPhysh said. "Sorry, Professor." He turned on his heel and walked to his waiting car.

I returned to my hotel in a despondent mood and began a dreary week of seeking employment. My friend arranged other interviews for me, some I made myself, but the results were always the same. No one appreciated my talents or the remarkable qualities of my bicycle. In this realm of fantasy they could see nothing especially unusual about it.

My final humiliation came when a Director of one of the lesser companies, specializing in vulgar low-class comedies, offered me employment, but without my bicycle!

My golden dreams of a Hollywood career melted away as rapidly as my money. When I paid my hotel bill at the end of the week my finances were sadly depleted. I decided then and there that I had had enough of Hollywood.

My friend came to see me off and informed me that the lovely Gloria Glamora was "working on location" as it was called, near Las Vegas, Nevada, so I decided to stop there on my homeward journey.

I left Hollywood without regret, and without my new sport jacket which, unfortunately, had been purloined.

A few hot and dusty days brought me to the vicinity of Las Vegas where I easily located the motion picture company's camp. The heat was so terrific that I could not have stayed on the earth had I wished to. Riding at considerable height I could see the tents, trailers, cars, mess shacks and a huge herd of cattle.

Close to the cattle I discerned a group of people, horsemen, trucks, generators, cameras and sound equipment. There, I felt sure, must also be the lovely Gloria Glamora and accordingly I turned my course in that direction. I had to pedal very hard to overcome the extreme buoyancy of my tires.

Unfortunately the sight of me and my bicycle with its gay umbrella passing overhead caused great consternation among the cattle. Suddenly the immense herd started a wild stampede directly toward the unfortunate picture people.

The cowardly horsemen scattered in all directions, leaving one slight feminine figure, atop a magnificent stallion, alone and helpless in the path of the thundering herd.

The horse began to run aimlessly; the rider, obviously no horsewoman, had lost her reins and clung desperately to the pommel.

Pedaling like mad I swooped low, grasped the reins and with the greatest effort managed to swing the terrified steed out of the path of the onrushing doom.

Of course the lone figure was the gorgeous Gloria Glamora, but in the hot glare of the desert sun how differently she appeared from that seductive apparition which had so often entranced me from the screen of the Bijou Theater!

She had lost her sombrero, and with it a great part of her hair. The remainder hung in lank rattails about her face, now streaked with running make-up. And she was sweating profusely, a condition which has always struck me as most unconducive to feminine charm.

But if her appearance was disillusioning, her voice was shattering. Those deep, dulcet, beguiling tones became now the harsh screech of an angry macaw.

And her language! In my travels abroad I have occasionally heard exchanges between Billingsgate fishwives, but these were the mere prattlings of innocent children compared to the flood of invective that was loosed on me.

"At least, Madame," I finally managed to put in, "at least I have saved your life."

"So what?" she snarled.

Sadly I mounted my bicycle and prepared to take off. "So I have done a great wrong to the motion picture public," I replied with what dignity I could summon. I thereupon departed, my last Hollywood illusion completely laid in the dust.

After these bitter disappointments, the quiet life of the campus seemed most appealing, and since my classes would be resuming in a short time I decided to turn my course homeward. There was only one more spot in the West which I still wished to visit, this being the famed Yellowstone Park.

Since the great Boulder Dam lay in my direct route I stopped there and found it truly impressive. I rode across the dam several times which, of course, was no unusual feat; thousands of motorists have done it. I did, however, make my performance somewhat different by suddenly turning, when halfway across, and riding up the entire length of Lake Mead, a rather beautiful body of water.

This caused no little excitement among the tourists atop the dam.

The route from here to the Yellowstone traversed extremely mountainous country and I would have found it difficult traveling had it not been for a most unusual occurrence.

I was, of course, camping out nights and often supplemented my canned diet with fresh fish, of which I am very fond. I had brought along a light fly rod and now and then when crossing some mountain lake would drop my line, invariably being rewarded by one or two trout, or "speckled beauties" as they are sometimes called.

On this particular occasion I had just hooked a particularly fine trout, which I was having considerable trouble in landing, when it was suddenly seized by an enormous osprey, or fish hawk. The huge bird set off in a northeasterly direction, towing me at terrific speed.

Determined not to lose my line, I played the great hawk with all my skill, but he was equally determined and the battle continued for hours. It was not until late afternoon that the fish finally broke under the strain and so I was able to come down to earth. The portion of trout remaining to me was hardly edible, but I was delighted to find that the flight had carried me over all the most rugged part of the terrain, so I could hardly resent the loss of that one trout.

Yellowstone Park surpassed all my expectations. The scenery, the geysers and the steaming pools were most interesting and these beautiful hot water pools gave me an opportunity to do some much needed laundry work.

However, while engaged in this a near-calamity occurred. I had just finished rinsing the last of my underwear when, glancing around, I discovered an enormous bear chewing the rear tire of my bicycle! (I later discovered that I had ridden over a sticky candy bar, which doubtless was what attracted him.)

Whether it was my frantic approach or the odor of escaping Z-Gas which drove him away I do not know, but as I drew near the great beast rose on his haunches and after a few growls reluctantly withdrew.

I hastily snatched out my First Aid kit and applied some adhesive tape to the punctured tire, praying that not too much of the precious gas had been lost, but the rear tire seemed alarmingly soft.

I was now in what is often described as a "pretty pickle," for the rear wheel had lost most of its buoyancy while the front wheel still retained all its original lifting power, completely upsetting the equilibrium of my bicycle.

When I attempted to mount the front wheel rose straight up in the air while the rear one remained on the ground, much in the manner of a rearing horse. I have often seen trick bicyclists in the circus or in vaudeville ride in this manner, but to one unused to it it is most upsetting.

However, I could make some slight progress and eventually managed to reach a Service Station. Here I borrowed a piece of rubber tubing used for inflating tires and by connecting the valves of my front and rear tires was able to equalize their pressure.

While this restored the equilibrium of my bicycle, I was depressed to discover that the loss of gas had greatly reduced its buoyancy. Even in the heat of the midday sun I was scarcely able to rise more than a foot or so above the ground.

DO NOT FEED
THE BEARS

RL

I shall not dwell long on my homeward journey, for it was extremely dull. No longer could I leap great distances into the air, soaring over anything which impeded my progress. No longer could I skim through ugly or uninteresting country at the speed of the wind.

I was an eagle with clipped wings, tied to the earth almost as much as the ordinary bicyclist or motorist.

The rolling wheat fields of South Dakota and Iowa, while doubtless an excellent place to grow the nation's supply of wheat, were not particularly inspiring. Only the fact that there was a strong hot wind, which blew continuously, enabled me to pass through them with any degree of speed.

As I reached the Middle West I was driven to all sorts of humiliating expedients to hasten my journey. Sometimes, on payment of a small fee, I was allowed to hitch on behind a trailer truck for a day, a most uncomfortable mode of travel.

At other times I even took trains, with my bicycle securely chained down in the baggage car. This, however, proved too great a strain on my dwindling financial resources and I again took to the road.

This latter portion of my trip has been more than tiresome, but I am now cheered by the fact that within two or three days I will be at home. *Home is the sailor, home from the sea* (Stevenson). Next week my classes resume and I feel quite sure that by now Mrs. McWhinney will have recovered from her needlework enthusiasm and become more companionable. Altogether a very pleasant and restful prospect.

Also, there is the reassuring thought that in my laboratory there is a large tank of Z-Gas, worth, I should say, many thousands of dollars. You wouldn't care for ten dollars' worth?

❈   ❈   ❈

"No," Mr. Purslane answered, "I don't think I would."

"Five?" the Professor asked. "Because of your intelligent listening and pleasant hospitality, I would be delighted to supply you with a liter of this remarkable gas for the sum of five dollars. Think of the fun you could have with it."

Mr. Purslane had already been thinking of the fun he could have with it and it seemed well worth the price. He extracted a five-dollar bill from his wallet and passed it over.

The Professor accepted it with great dignity and stuck it in the band of the tall hat. "This," he said, "will enable me to complete my journey with a reasonable degree of comfort."

From inside the hat he drew a sheet of paper and a fountain pen and wrote out a very legally worded receipt. This promised to deliver to Charles Purslane, Esq., for value received, 1 cu. liter of Z-Gas, all shipping charges prepaid. It was signed Ambrose Augustus McWhinney, B.G.E., F.R.G.S., B.P.O.E., E.R.P., B.S. Cantab., G.H.Q., O.E.D. (Oxon.), etc.

With a deep bow and further expressions of gratitude he mounted his bicycle and rode down the Purslane driveway. There is a low stone wall beside this drive where it turns toward the main road and as a final gesture the Professor pedaled briskly, leaned back in the saddle, pulled up on the handle bars and just managed to clear the wall. He landed safely on the main road and disappeared down the hill.

That was a month or two ago and Mr. Purslane is still eagerly awaiting the arrival of the Z-Gas, for he has thought of a great many amusing things that could be done with such a remarkable substance.

It is probable that the Professor has been too busy with his new classes to get around to it. It is also just possible that, being somewhat absent-minded, he has forgotten all about it.